# YIKES!

## In Seven Wild Adventures,
## Who Would You Be?

# Alison Lester

Houghton Mifflin Company
Boston 1995

**In a Raging Storm at Sea...**

**...who would you be?**

Salty Scott, the captain,
trying to bring his ship around?

La Cantina singing
in a clinging velvet gown?

Sparrow Cripps, the cabin boy,
skinny, small and shy?

Or Jack the Stirrer rolling out
the pastry for a pie?

Bragging of the sharks he's slaughtered,
Blood and Guts McCoy?

The baby heiress playing
with a pearl-encrusted toy?

Sparky on his crackling wireless,
calling S.O.S?

Or Lady Clair St. Martin
and her favorite racehorse, Bess?

The captain sings a love song as he goes down with his ship,
to the overweight soprano who has made the lifeboat tip.
The cabin boy's a hero, he's pulled a dozen in,
while Jack the Stirrer floats away astride a cookie tin.

The sharks have called it even with Blood and Guts McCoy,
and the richest baby in the world is bobbing like a buoy.
Sparky perches on a rock to send an orange flare,
but the Lady and her thoroughbred have vanished—who knows where?

Billie Jo Coyote
with a saddlebag of gold?

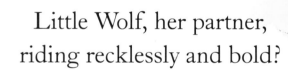

Little Wolf, her partner,
riding recklessly and bold?

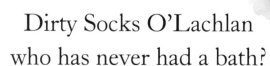

Dirty Socks O'Lachlan
who has never had a bath?

Or Tracker Eddy following
a cougar down the path?

Bad and Sins, the Evil Twins,
who ride with Dirty Socks?

The smiling Spanish dancer,
as silent as a fox?

Perhaps you'd be the sheriff
riding shotgun on the coach?

Or Shuffling Sal, the card shark,
showing off her diamond brooch?

Little Wolf leaps fearlessly to stop the horses bolting,
and the cougar gnaws O'Lachlan, though the smell is quite revolting.
Billie spurs her buckskin mare across the yawning gap,
and Tracker Eddy dangles from his own ingenious trap.

A rattlesnake surprises Bad—one twitch and he'll be dead.

For target practice, Sal shoots the sombrero off his head.

The sheriff drops a rope round Sins, but when the dust has cleared,

the dancer and the priceless diamond brooch have disappeared.

**Under the Big Top...** ...who would you be?

The Flying Fabuloso,
hurtling through space?

Straight and steady on the highwire,
Anti-Matter Grace?

Trixie Ryder, bareback
on her famous dapple-grays?

Or the daring Human Cannonball
who's seen far better days?

Vesuvius breathing fireballs
from his badly blistered lips?

Atlas striding powerfully
with seven on his hips?

Lenny Little trembling
in the corner of the cage?

Or Catra, lashing desperately
to curb the leopards' rage?

Fabuloso's missed his swing and heads towards disaster,
but the Cannonball flicks out a rope when he goes falling past her.
Vesuvius makes a wall of fire to keep the cats at bay,
and a pyramid of sturdy dwarves helps Atlas save the day.

Distracted, Grace slips off the wire and tumbles like a leaf,
but breaks her fall on Trixie's grays as they trot underneath.
Little Len is safe, although his trousers have a rip,
but all that's left of Catra is her silver-handled whip.

# In the Frozen North...

## ...who would you be?

Missing Toes O'Reilly
on a lone prospecting trip?

Annie Black, the cowgirl,
and her baby brother, Pip?

Shifty Jackson racing
with a meager load of pelts?

Or Willy, keen to beat him home
before the crossing melts?

Georgia Swift, the Mountie,
tracking down her man?

A hard, embittered contract killer
known as Deadly Dan?

Maddy Waters whistling
as she paddles down the stream?

Or the lost and frozen traveller,
trying not to scream?

The traveller sees a friendly light—he stumbles drawn and grim
up to O'Reilly's campfire, but the wolves are closing in.
Deadly Dan lines up his man and starts to squeeze the trigger,
but Georgia's headlock brings him down—she's faster and much bigger.

As Willy crashes through the ice his huskies race ahead,
but Maddy drags him out before he's frozen blue and dead.
Annie grabs a burning branch to drive away the pack,
And Shifty Jackson's gone, although his laughter echoes back.

**Beyond the Milky Way...**  ...who would you be?

Commander Sarah Stardust,
out to save the human race?

Riptide, with his lifeline broken,
spinning off in space?

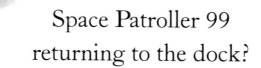

Space Patroller 99
returning to the dock?

Or Professor Fuzzy Logic
with a strangely ticking rock?

U.R.2, the robot,
rocking robo-quads to sleep?

Evil Lord Sukpeepolup
emerging from the deep?

The Master of the Aliens,
advancing with his horde?

Or the trans-galactic bus conductor,
Carburetta Claude?

99 is decimating aliens with her laser.
Stardust fights beside her with a parabolic phaser.
While U.R.2's extending arm locks to the Mother Ship,
his human-sensing safety line locates and rescues Rip.

Claude tumbles off the spacebus in a shower of meteors,
to be ambushed by Sukpeepolup and forced between his jaws.
The rock explodes and drives the aliens back to outer space—
Fuzzy Logic threw it, now he's gone without a trace.

**In a Steaming Jungle...**

...who would you be?

Princess Sweet Bananas
wearing hand-embroidered silk?

Little Toot, her brother,
with the sugar, tea and milk?

Jamshed riding Trunky
through the rushing mountain stream?

Or Lily Pott, the painter,
in a Technicolor dream?

The leader of the bandits
with a knife between his teeth?

Playing on his magic flute,
the cobra-charmer, Keith?

Ali-Ba, the jewel thief,
sneaking off with Lily's gold?

Or the animal photographer
wondering why his back feels cold?

The bandits leap from hiding, but a tiger brings one down,
and Toot knocks out another with his sister's silver crown.
Trunky plucks Bananas from the wildly swinging bridge,
and Ali-Ba, the jewel thief, meets a python on the ridge.

When Lily wakes, a hissing snake strikes terror in her soul,
but Keith the charmer plays a tune and lures it to his bowl.
The photographer has taken an extraordinary snap,
but Jamshed isn't in it—just his slowly sinking cap.

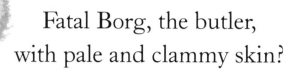

Fatal Borg, the butler,
with pale and clammy skin?

Gory Lipp, the housemaid, saying
"Darlings, do come in!"?

Ernestine and Thomas,
sent to stay the night?

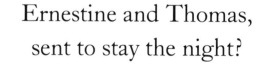

Or Helmut with his dribbling hound
that seems inclined to bite?

Long-dead Cousin Wilma,
howling in the hall?

Farty Schmits, the hunchback,
climbing up the wall?

Segundo Hand who's friendly,
despite his scars and stitches?

or Little Min and Warty Nose,
two antiquated witches?

When Fatal Borg reveals his fangs and threatens to attack,
young Ernestine whips out her cross and sends him reeling back.
Thomas grabs his pointy stick as Gory nears the bed,
and pokes it in her wicked heart to kill the vampire dead.

Farty Schmits, the hunchback, slips and plummets through the night,
while Little Min and Warty get their witchy mixture right.
Helmut and his hound are chasing Wilma to the wood,
but Segundo Hand has disappeared, presumably for good.

# And here's what happened...

Bess swam bravely through the waves,
and Lady Clair clung tight.
They struggled in the foaming seas
for two days and a night.

The ocean finally washed them up
along the Ivory Coast,
where Clair trains polo ponies,
but she still loves Bess the most.

The Spanish dancer stole the brooch,
determined to be wealthy,
but money can't buy happiness,
or even keep you healthy.

Despite a life of luxury,
she started feeling queer.
The brooch was an unlucky one—
she died within a year.

Catra felt a coward
leaving Lenny to his plight,
but her nerves were shot to pieces
and she couldn't sleep at night.

She went to live a wholesome life,
avoiding sweets and fats,
and ran a home for lost dogs,
having always hated cats.

Shifty thought he'd pulled a swifty,
stealing Willy's sled.
He'd seen his rival crashing
and assumed that he'd be dead.

"This pile of pelts will make me rich,"
he yelled, "I'll be the winner!"
but down the track a grumpy grizzly
guzzled him for dinner.

Outer Space is dangerous—
the going can get rough.
Professor Fuzzy Logic
finally knew he'd had enough.

He hopped aboard a spacebike
and headed back to Mars,
where he hosts a television show
explaining quarks and stars.

When Jamshed lost his balance
and the current swept him south,
Bananas pulled him out half-drowned
and gave him mouth-to-mouth.

From that moment it was obvious
they were made to love each other,
so they rode away on Trunky,
waving farewell to her brother.

Segundo, as it happened,
was a most unusual man.
He could take out both his eyeballs
and disconnect his hand.

He left the haunted castle,
where everyone was mean,
and became the greatest conjurer
the world has ever seen.

THE END

For Joan and Eric

*Library of Congress Cataloging-in-Publication Data*

Lester, Alison.
 Yikes! : in seven wild adventures, who would you be? / Alison Lester. — 1st American ed.
  p. cm.
 "Originally published in Australia in 1993 by Allen & Unwin" — T.p. verso.
 Summary: seven rhyming adventures, from a raging storm at sea to a Transylvanian castle,
 each with a zany cast of eight characters.
 ISBN 0-395-71252-1
 [1. Adventure and adventurers — Fiction. 2. Stories in rhyme.] I. Title.
     PZ8.3.L54935Yi  1995                94-10508
     [E] — dc20                          CIP
                                         AC

Printed in in Australia by Pirie Printers Pty Ltd
10 9 8 7 6 5 4 3 2 1